where do Stars come from, Nana?

Tina Perry

TATE PUBLISHING & Enterprises

Published by Tate Publishing & Enterprises, LLC
127 E. Trade Center Terrace | Mustang, Oklahoma 73064 USA
1.888.361.9473 | www.tatepublishing.com

Tate Publishing is committed to excellence in the publishing industry. The company reflects the philosophy established by the founders, based on Psalms 68:11,
 "The Lord gave the word and great was the company of those who published it."

Published in the United States of America

ISBN: 978-1-6024707-0-5
07.06.06

Bobby, thank you for always being there for our family. I am so blessed to be able to say I married my best friend. Even after 27 years of marriage, I still enjoy our talks. Words can only affirm what my heart has known since the 7th grade—I love you.

Author's Note

The book being discussed in the story is the Holy Bible and verses used to make up the story line are: Psalms 8:3; Isaiah 40:12; Matthew 2:2, 9; Psalms 147:4.

It was my intent that the answers the Grandparents in the story gave lined up with the Word of God. Thank you and may God richly bless you and your family.

Tina Perry

This Book Belongs To:

_____

It was the last day of school. At Nana and Papa's house, the RV was ready. The swimsuits were packed. It was time to pick up Hunter from school.

Hunter waited outside the school on a bench. His excitement grew with every minute. Nana and Papa were picking him up from school today. They were taking him on his first camping trip.

When the RV stopped, Hunter ran over to it.

"Hi, Nana and Papa," Hunter called.

"Hi, Hunter," Nana and Papa said at the same time.

"Ready for our campout?" Papa asked Hunter.

"Don't forget you said we could look for frogs," Hunter reminded Papa.

"I haven't forgotten," Papa said.

The campsite was only a short distance away. But as they drove, the sun seemed to disappear.

"Why did it get dark so fast?" Hunter asked Papa.

"The trees are shading us from the sun," Papa answered. "You'll notice things will look different out here than at home. Look, Hunter. There's the campsite sign. Let's pull in and find a spot to park the RV."

"Let's park over there," Hunter pointed, "under those trees."

"I think that will be perfect," Nana said. "Let's set up camp."

Hunter was a good helper. He helped Nana set up the table and chairs. He helped Papa hang lights on the RV. He even helped carry firewood to the fire pit.

"Thanks for your help, Hunter," Nana said. "Do you want to swim while I fix something to eat?"

"No, I am ready to look for frogs," Hunter said.

"It's not dark enough," Papa said.

"How much longer do we have to wait?" Hunter asked.

"It will be dark enough once the stars come out," answered Papa.

Hunter plopped down next to the pit and said, "Stars are boring. All they do is hang in space and shine."

"Stars are very important, Hunter," said Nana.

"What's so great about them? Do you know where stars come from, Nana?" Hunter asked.

"Yes, God used His fingers to put the stars in place,"
Nana replied.

"His fingers?" Looking down at his hands, Hunter
said, "God must have big hands."

"I read that He can hold the oceans in His hand,"
Nana said.

"That is a big hand. I wonder how many frogs He
can hold?" Turning toward Papa, Hunter asked, "Is it
time to go hunt frogs yet?"

"Almost," Papa answered.

"Nana, do you know how many stars there are?"

"No, but God does. He even knows each
star's name, too."

"Stars have names?" Hunter asked
with a puzzled look on his face.

"Yes, I read a book that says God
named each one."

"Why did God make the stars?"

"Before there were cars, people used to travel places by ships and other boats. The ship's captain read the stars like we would read a map. One of the most important reasons God made the stars was to lead the wise men to Baby Jesus when He was born. One star lit bright in the sky for many weeks so they wouldn't lose their way," said Nana.

"Is that why people use telescopes, to find Jesus?" Hunter asked.

"Some people enjoy looking through telescopes at what God created," Papa answered.

"Then there are other people that love stars more than God," said Nana.

"Are there really people that love stars more than God?" Hunter asked.

"I'm afraid so," Nana said.

"Shouldn't we all love God, Papa?"

"Yes, it's up to you and me to help those that are confused," Papa answered.

Jumping up quickly, Hunter tilted his head toward the stream, "Did you hear that, Papa?"

"Yes, I heard," answered Papa. "It sounds like the frogs are out now. Let's go and get our flashlights."

The two frog hunters began their search. Walking away from the camp, the trees cleared.

Pointing toward the sky, Hunter said, "Look at all those stars. There must be millions of them. Did you know that God knows every one of the star's names?"

Before Papa could answer, Hunter took off running toward the stream. "Hurry Papa," Hunter yelled. "There's a frog. We don't want it to get away."

Bending over the stream, Hunter noticed the stars shining in the water.

Papa walked up behind Hunter and asked, "Did you find the frog?"

"Papa, why aren't the stars this bright at my house?"

"There are too many lights in town. When the street-lights, car lights, and business signs all shine at the same time, the stars seem to lose their brightness."

Looking up at the sky, Hunter said, "Papa I don't think stars are boring anymore. Nana's right, stars really are important. I wonder if there's anything in that Book Nana read about frogs?"

"Let's ask Nana when we get back to camp," Papa suggested.

Papa and Hunter walked down the stream before making their way back to camp. Hunter was glad he learned about the stars on his first night camping out.

The End

e|LIVE

listen|imagine|view|experience

AUDIO BOOK DOWNLOAD INCLUDED WITH THIS BOOK!

In your hands you hold a complete digital entertainment package. Besides purchasing the paper version of this book, this book includes a free download of the audio version of this book. Simply use the code listed below when visiting our website. Once downloaded to your computer, you can listen to the book through your computer's speakers, burn it to an audio CD or save the file to your portable music device (such as Apple's popular iPod) and listen on the go!

How to get your free audio book digital download:

1. Visit www.tatepublishing.com and click on the e|LIVE logo on the home page.
2. Enter the following coupon code:
    a1cb-d809-a3ea-0704-e68e-0cfe-d2c1-1e49
3. Download the audio book from your e|LIVE digital locker and begin enjoying your new digital entertainment package today!